THE JERSEY

NO GIRLY-GIRLS ALLOWED!

NO GIRLY-GIRLS ALLOWED!

Adapted by Jay Sinclair
Based on the series created by Gordon Korman

CHANNEL

New York

First Edition
1 3 5 7 9 10 8 6 4 2

Library of Congress Catalog Card Number: 00-100796

ISBN 0-7868-4422-1
For more Disney Press fun, visit www.disneybooks.com

CONTENTS

CHAPTER ONE

SPLASHDOWN!

Morgan adjusted her bike helmet and watched as her cousin Nick sped off along the dirt road on his BMX bike. Nick picked up speed as he pedaled, eventually reaching the top of the hill. Then he took off and flew into the sky.

"Look at me! I'm an air god!" he screamed as he leaped.

Not to be outdone, Nick's buddy, Coleman, picked up speed, leaping off the mound close behind Nick. "Superman!" Coleman shouted as he took off from the hill, lifted his feet off his bike pedals, and lay flat across the frame of the bike. He flew through the air looking a lot like a flying super hero.

Morgan, the only girl in the group of BMX daredevils, was not the kind of female who would be outdone by the guys. She was every bit as much of a daredevil as they were—in fact, maybe even more so. She quickly picked up speed, and pedaled up to the top of an even higher hill.

"GRAVITY SHATTERS!" she bellowed as she shot her bike straight up in the air.

By the time Morgan hit the ground, Coleman and Nick were already off on a new BMX track, climbing ever higher past mud puddles and through thick dirt. Morgan picked up the pace to join them. Morgan, Coleman, and Nick were so engrossed in their race to the top of the hill that they hardly even noticed that their buddy Elliott—who was not exactly known for his athletic prowess—was trailing far behind.

Nick and Morgan were cousins. They'd been buddies ever since they were babies. But that didn't keep them from competing with each other every chance they got. Like now. Nick hit the top of the the highest hill at the dirt BMX track, and soared off doing a 360° spin on his bike before landing below. "Eat my dust!" he called up to Morgan.

No problem. Morgan followed her cousin's lead, flew off the top of the hill, and did a 360° as well.

"Show-offs," Coleman called down to both of his buddies as he rode, leaping off the hill to join them. Elliott followed behind, biking down hill instead of leaping. There was no way he was going to try a 360° spin in the air. Elliott was way too cautious for that—at least on a bike.

"Check it out," Nick told his pals as soon as they were all gathered at the foot of the hill. He leaned forward in his seat, and began pedaling his bike as hard as possible, gaining all the speed he could. "I'm gonna break the record," he vowed as he looked down at the mud puddle below. Nick, Morgan, and Coleman often had contests to see who could jump over the largest mud puddle without landing in the thick, gooey stuff.

Morgan looked at the puddle. It was huge. She wasn't so sure Nick could clear it. But Nick seemed absolutely positive that he could. He leaped off the hill, soared through the air, and totally cleared the mud puddle. But his joy was extremely short-lived. When Nick's bike did finally hit land, it came down smack in the middle of an even bigger mud puddle than the one he'd tried to jump.

The bike plopped into the mud pile with a huge force. Mud rocketed all over the place. The shock caused Nick to lose his bearings. He fell off his bike and right into the mud.

A group of teenage girls and their boyfriends gathered around Nick as he sat up and wiped the thick black-brown sludge from his face. The girls giggled and their boyfriends laughed hysterically. Nick could feel his face turning red beneath the dark mud mask. He looked sheepishly to his friends for help.

"What are they laughing at?" Nick moaned with embarrassment as Morgan, Elliott, and Coleman waded into the mud and helped Nick to his feet.

"Don't worry about them. We know we're cool," Morgan assured her cousin as she righted his bike and pulled it onto firmer ground.

"Yeah, who needs 'em?" Coleman agreed.

"I don't care what those girls think," Elliott added.

"Me neither," Nick said. But he didn't sound as convincing as the others had. After all, they hadn't been the ones the girls had been laughing at. And not just any girls—older girls, and their boyfriends. Nick had just looked like a total jerk in front of all of them!

SPLASHDOWN!

"Exactly," Morgan told the guys. "My opinion is the only one that matters."

Nick, Coleman, and Elliott just stared at Morgan. Was she serious?

"Kidding," she assured the guys as she raised her hand for a high five.

As Nick slapped his cousin's hand, he gave her a wink of gratitude. Her joke had definitely lightened the situation. Nick was really glad Morgan had moved to town from Chicago. And he was thrilled that she liked hanging around with him and his buds. It certainly wasn't every girl who liked to sit around on Monday nights and watch football games. But Morgan was a welcome addition to the Monday Night Football Club (or MNFC, for short)—of which Nick, Coleman, and Elliott were the only other members. Nick had formed the club so he and his friends could be guaranteed that they would watch all the Monday Night Football games, together. They met Mondays at Nick's house, ate pizza, drank soda, and watched the game.

If Morgan had been a really girly-girl, the kind who only care about reading fan magazines, wearing makeup, and shopping at the mall for hours, it would have been hard for Nick and her to have gotten so close. But Morgan seemed to like everything the guys did. That made it easy for Nick and her to hang out together.

Besides, if Nick really wanted to admit it, he would have to say that Morgan was at least as good an athlete as he was. Maybe even better at some sports. Take soccer. She'd only been at the local junior high for a few months, and already Morgan was the lead scorer on the her team. And like Nick and his friends, Morgan was only a ninth grader! Nick didn't know anyone—girl or guy—who could claim something like that.

All of that made it easy for Nick to trust Morgan with the MNFC's biggest secret—a magic football jersey that had been left to Nick by his grandfather when he died.

At first Nick had not been too thrilled to have been willed a ratty, old, scratchy woolen football jersey. But then he had discovered the secret of the magic jersey: if you put the jersey on at just the right time, you became a famous sports star. The trouble was, you never knew when the right time was.

Nick himself had already entered the body of football players Charles Woodson and Steve Young.

THE JERSEY

Being inside a pro sports player's body was just about the most amazing experience any sports fan could imagine. But it was also a huge responsibility to that player's teammates. After all, they never knew it was really just a kid inside there. Only the biggest sports fans could be trusted with a job like that. And Nick's cousin Morgan was one of them.

By the time Nick climbed back on his bike, Morgan was already well on the way up another hill on the BMX trail. She turned and gave Nick a look that dared him to beat her to the top. Nick pedaled harder. He couldn't let his cousin beat him! Not this time, anyway.

CHAPTER TWO

THE ABSOLUTE WORST DAY

The following afternoon, Morgan left the three male members of the MNFC on their own. She didn't have time to go BMX riding or throw around the football. Her soccer team had scheduled a practice—and Morgan had to be there.

"Look, I'm Mia Hamm!" Morgan called out to her teammates as she shuffled a soccer ball between her feet, and made her way over to the school's practice field. She pushed her red-brown bangs off her face and raced down the field in her best imitation of the professional forward who was the star of the 1999 Women's World Cup Games, not to mention the first three-time U.S. Soccer athlete of the year.

"Wait'll we're on defense," one of Morgan's teammates answered her. "Then I'll be Carla Overbeck."

Morgan laughed. Carla Overbeck was a champion defender. The team should be so lucky to have someone like her on their side. But, hey, even those pros had once been kids like Morgan and her teammates. Morgan wondered if Mia or Carla had ever been anything like her. Had they ever moved to a new town, where meeting new kids was scary? Had they ever had a cousin like Nick who they could practice their soccer saves with? Were they always so excited about soccer that it was all they ever thought about? Or were they more like Morgan, someone who loved any kind of sport, just as long as she could play with really good teammates?

It was kind of nice thinking about Mia and Carla being a little bit like her. It gave Morgan hope that maybe some day, she could be a professional athlete.

As much as Morgan liked the guys in the MNFC, it was nice being around girls who loved sports as much as she did. Not all girls did—not by a long shot. Some girls actually wore it as a badge of honor that they didn't know anything about sports. That was something Morgan couldn't understand. Why was ignorance a good thing? Didn't those girls know what they were missing out on?

But the girls on Morgan's team were totally into soccer. And like Morgan, they searched the newspapers and magazines for any word on the U.S. soccer teams, and hung posters of the top players on their walls. Morgan felt lucky to have found a group of girls like that to hang with.

As Morgan's soccer team neared the practice field, a soccer ball rolled up toward Morgan. She reached out her leg, and gave the ball a good, swift bicycle kick back on to the field. The ball rose up into the air and . . . *slam!* It hit a player on another team right in the back of the head.

The boy rubbed the back of his head, and slowly turned to see who had delivered the offending hit. Oh, no! Morgan thought as the boy revealed himself. It was that cute kid Ryan, from Mrs. Hogan's class!

From the minute Ryan turned around to face her, Morgan was mortified. How could she ever have kicked the ball right into the head of such an adorable guy?! Her face turned beet red and she could feel the heat of her embarrassment flying off of her skin. This was the kind of thing a boy like that would remember forever— and it was the kind of moment Morgan wished she could forget. Better yet, she wished she could turn back the clock by about thirty seconds, so this would never have even occurred. "Oops, sorry," she apologized as she blushed furiously and tugged nervously at one of her long brown braids. "Really . . . sorry . . . uh . . . I . . ."

Ryan smiled at Morgan. And for one

brief second, she seemed sure that he thought she was kind of cute, too. Maybe he even recognized her from science class. She'd seen him there before. He sat three rows behind her, but she had noticed him. A guy who looked like Ryan was hard to miss.

"No problem," Ryan assured her. "You're *Marilyn* right?"

Morgan's shoulder slumped slightly with disappointment. "Close," she told him, trying to muster a smile. "It's Morgan."

"From Mrs. Hogan's class, right?" Ryan asked her.

Morgan grinned and nodded. So he *did* remember.

"Well, hey, I needed to practice my head butt," he replied.

Morgan looked at him blankly. Ryan

smiled weakly, slightly surprised that Morgan didn't get the joke.

But apparently the other girls on the soccer team were tuned in to Ryan's sense of humor. They gathered around Ryan and giggled as though he had just told one of the funniest jokes in the history of the planet. Then one of Morgan's teammates batted her eyelashes in his direction and asked, "Ryan, are you okay? That had to hurt so much."

Ryan nodded. "I'm okay. Thanks, though."

As Ryan trotted back to practice, he flashed Morgan a smile. She returned the grin, and then went back to kicking her soccer ball back and forth. She was looking for someone to practice passing with, but suddenly, none of the other girls seemed to have soccer on their minds.

They were all gathered in a circle, talking about Ryan.

"He is one cute boy," the goalie remarked with a sigh.

"Babe-a-licious," agreed one of the defenders.

Morgan walked over to the circle of teammates and shook her head. "What is with you guys?" she demanded. Then she raised her voice high, so she sounded like a helpless little girl. "Oh, Ryan," she said, mocking her teammates. "You got hit with a ball. Let me save your life."

Morgan looked so funny, batting her eyelashes and smiling innocently up at the sky, they couldn't help but laugh— even though she was making fun of them. But they didn't really see what was so bizarre about their behavior. And that confused Morgan. She knew that she would be totally freaked out if anyone had ever caught her flirting as shamelessly as her teammates had with Ryan. On the outside, Morgan appeared triumphant and confident as she teased her friends. But on the inside, Morgan had to admit to feeling more than just a little inadequate. Morgan might be one great athlete, but she knew that when it came to dealing with boys, she was out of her league.

There was only one thing for Morgan to do. She was going to have to get some help from an expert. And there was only one girl in Morgan's circle of friends who knew just what to do to get a guy to notice you: her older cousin, Nick's sister, Hilary. Hilary was the queen of girly-girls. She knew what lip gloss went with what nail polish, which stores in the mall had the coolest clothes, and just how to do your hair to put your face in the best light.

Usually, Morgan, along with the rest of the Monday Night Football Club, laughed at Hilary. They couldn't understand her love of talking on the phone for hours, or trying new colors of eye shadow and lip gloss. And they especially couldn't understand her total hatred of anything involving sports—except, of course, the boys who played them.

If she had to choose between an afternoon with Hilary, listening to pop records and doing each other's nails, or trying out new football plays with the other members of the MNFC, Morgan would have chosen Nick, Elliott, and Coleman any day.

But today was different. Morgan needed help. And this was not something she was going to get from the guys. She

THE ABSOLUTE WORST DAY

had to go to the most knowledgeable person in the world when it came to getting along with boys—as more than just a pal. She had to talk to Hilary.

CHAPTER THREE

FLIRTING LESSONS

Late that afternoon, as soon as practice was over, Morgan hurried to her cousins' house, hoping to get to talk to Hilary before the rest of the MNFC arrived. The MNFC usually gathered at Nick and Hilary's house after they were done playing—supposedly to work together on their homework. (Of course, most afternoons they spent more time talking about athletes than they did algebra.)

Morgan wanted to talk to Hilary about Ryan. And she definitely didn't want the guys to find out that she had a crush on someone. She knew they would tease her mercilessly if they did. After all, the guys didn't exactly see her as a girl—they saw her as one of them. And Morgan had a feeling they would have a hard time accepting the fact that there was this whole other side of her. She didn't want them to freak out about it.

Luckily, Morgan managed to beat the guys to the house. She raced into the family room and caught Hilary walking across the room with an exaggerated wiggle of her rear end. She was watching her reflection in the mirror.

"What's up, Hil?" Morgan asked as she entered the room.

Surprisingly, Hilary wasn't at all embarrassed at being caught in the middle of doing such a funny, exaggerated walk. "Just getting into character," Hilary explained. "I'm Lola in *Damn Yankees*."

Morgan nodded. Hilary was always involved in one school play or another. At least this was one Morgan was familiar with. *Damn Yankees* was a musical about an ordinary guy named Joe who makes a deal with the devil so he can become a great baseball player. Lola was the lead female character in the play. She was one of the devil's helpers—the kind of girl who always got her man—thanks to her beauty and charm. Lola was the ultimate flirt.

"Joe, you want to play baseball and win?" Hilary asked her imaginary costar in a soft, deep, breathy, French-sounding voice. Then she looked to Morgan for approval of the way she had just spoken her line from the show.

Morgan hadn't really been paying attention, but she figured Hilary expected her to say something. So she answered simply, "That sounded really good."

Hilary beamed. But before Hilary could try any more dialogue out on her, Morgan decided to change the subject. After all, it wouldn't be long before the boys got there. And she really needed Hilary's advice.

"Uh, Hil, I've got to ask you something that probably sounds dopey, but just listen before you fall on the floor laughing," Morgan said to her cousin.

"I'm fascinated," Hilary replied sincerely. She sat on the couch and wrapped her arms around her knees. "What?"

Morgan stood up and paced around the room, avoiding Hilary's stare. It would be too hard to ask Hil this one face-to-face. She finally began, nervously. "So say there was this guy . . ."

"How do you get him to notice you?" Hilary butted in, saving Morgan the embarrassment of having to say it herself.

"Yeah," Morgan replied with relief. "Exactly. It's sort of a new problem for me."

Hilary grinned. "First crush? Welcome to the world of womanhood."

Morgan scowled. She hated it when older girls like Hilary made fun of her. Morgan was really serious about this. "Thanks. Now what do I do?"

Hilary laughed. "It's easy. You smile, look them in the eye, and laugh at their stupid jokes. All guys think they're funny."

Morgan looked confused. That didn't

make any sense. "But why would I laugh if it's stupid?"

"So they'll notice you," Hil explained. She looked at her younger cousin and sighed. Morgan may have been a star on the soccer field, playing like someone years older than she really was. But when it came to social situations that did not involve a ball, a goal cage, and a scoreboard, she was pretty far behind most other girls. Hilary was glad her cousin had come to her. Ever since Morgan had moved to town, she'd liked having another girl around the house. And it would be even more fun to have another girl around who liked the things Hilary did. In Hilary's mind, if Morgan discovered boys, she would just naturally have less time for jumping mud puddles on her BMX, and more time for painting her nails and putting on makeup with Hilary. Yes, Hilary figured she was really going to enjoy teaching Morgan the ABCs of flirting.

Just then Coleman and Elliott walked in and interrupted the conversation. "What's going on?" Elliott asked.

Morgan cringed. Hilary wouldn't tell the guys about this, would she?

"I'm teaching Morgan what real boys like. Maybe the two of you should take notes."

Yup, Hilary would.

Morgan blushed angrily. She couldn't believe her older cousin had betrayed her confidence. "This could've been between you and me," she hissed in Hilary's ear.

But Hilary didn't seem to notice Morgan's discomfort. She kept on explaining her philosophy on boys. "The male ego is extremely fragile. You should never threaten it, because it's all guys have. And they need to feel big and strong." She turned to Coleman and Elliott. "So if you're a little weaker . . ."

"That's not true," Coleman insisted.

Hilary laughed. "Excuse me. We're talking about mature boys, like juniors in high school. Not you guys." And with that, Hilary left and walked into the kitchen. Morgan followed close behind anxiously, to hear what her older, more experienced cousin had to say.

Morgan wasn't the only one who wanted to hear Hilary's pearls of wisdom. Elliot and Coleman were curious, too. So they decided now would be good time to get themselves a snack.

Which left the family room completely empty, except for the magic jersey Nick kept on the bookshelf. That thing seemed to have a life of its own at times. And apparently, this was one of those times. As soon as the room was empty, the jersey appeared to move. Slowly at first, gingerly making its way down from the bookshelf to the floor. Then it picked up speed, using its empty blue arms to creep and crawl across the floor and into Morgan's backpack. It was almost as though the jersey was possessed by a ghost. It would have totally creeped the members of the MNFC out, had any of them actually been there to see it, but nobody was in the room at the time.

They were all in the kitchen. Elliott was busy refuting Hilary's claims that he and Coleman were totally immature. Elliott stood up tall—which wasn't very tall at all, since Elliott was kind of short. "I'm extremely mature," he informed

Hilary. "My grandma always tells people that."

"Oh, really?" Hilary asked. "Okay, let's ask your girlfriend. Oops, you don't have one. Wonder why? Morgan, all you have to do is pretend that guys are great at everything, and pretend that you could never be as good as they are."

Morgan stared at Hilary in amazement. She couldn't believe that her cousin was asking her to act like some sort of idiot princess just to get a guy to like her. But that was exactly what she was doing.

"You don't have to be stupid about it," Hil continued. "It's subtle. A smile. Then 'Oooh, could you help me?' or maybe 'Wow! could you teach me . . . some soccer thing or something.'"

Morgan shook her head. That didn't make any sense at all. Why would she have to ask Ryan for help with soccer? "But I play way better than Ryan," she explained to her older cousin.

Hil looked at the sky and rubbed her frazzled brow in frustration. Morgan was obviously not getting the point. "But do you have to rub his nose in it? Or do you want him to be putty in your hands to mold as you please?"

Morgan was getting a little angry. It wasn't fair of Hilary to treat her like she was a five-year-old. The way Hilary was talking to her made Morgan feel stupid. And the worst part about it was that Hilary was doing it in front of her friends. And she was using Morgan's plea for advice to make fun of Morgan's pals, Coleman and Elliott. Morgan knew Hilary didn't particularly like Nick's male friends (in fact she sometimes called the

MNFC the Monday Night Freak Club) but this was really just too much.

Still, Morgan knew she would have to put up with Hilary's less-than-subtle ways if she was ever going to get a guy like Ryan to notice her as anything other than a walking soccer accident.

Hilary handed Morgan the laundry basket and promised, "Help me with the laundry and I will reveal more."

As the girls left the room, Coleman and Elliott looked at each other nervously. Morgan liked a guy! *An outsider.* That meant things were going to change. She might be starting out with this boy. Playing sports with him. Even watching football games with him. Coleman and Elliott were suddenly worried that this could be the end of MNFC. There was only one thing for them to do.

"If Morgan's starting to like a guy, then girls should like us," Coleman told Elliott.

"What girls?"

Coleman shrugged. "I don't know. There must be some. Somewhere. We just have to find them."

CHAPTER FOUR

THE DECISION

Morgan didn't have to wait long to find out if Hilary's advice worked. The very next day, Morgan's soccer team was scheduled to play against Ryan's.

As Morgan approached the field, she spotted a group of girls surrounding Ryan. He was telling a joke, and the girls were laughing hard, just like Hilary would have.

"That's a good one," one of the defenders

said as she edged closer to Ryan's side. Morgan watched as she tilted her head just slightly in Ryan's direction—as though she were dying to hear his next word—another of the tricks Hilary had taught Morgan.

Hilary had instructed Morgan to pretend that Ryan was just the most interesting person she had ever met, and that everything he had to say was simply fascinating. Watching her teammates interact with Ryan made Morgan wonder who they had gotten their flirting advice from. Or did it just come naturally to some girls?

"Where do you come up with these?" one of the forwards echoed her teammate's praise of Ryan's comedic talents.

Ryan was beaming. He was eating up the girls' reactions. "I know 'em all," he bragged.

THE DECISION

"You could be a stand-up comedian," a girl goalie assured Ryan with a perfectly straight face.

Morgan watched the whole thing with amazement. Hilary's plan had sounded so bizarre. But standing here, watching the girls flirt with Ryan—and watching Ryan's reaction to their flirting—Morgan had to admit that maybe her older cousin knew what she was talking about.

Morgan's mind just wasn't on the game that afternoon. Even as she warmed up, she kept one eye on Ryan—until she noticed he was looking back at her. Then she blushed and ran out onto the field.

In the final quarter, the score was tied. Morgan managed to control the ball and take it straight down the field, steering clear of the other team's defensive players. Finally, she had a clear path to their goal.

She pulled her leg back and prepared to whack one into the net. But then, out of the corner of her eye, she saw Ryan running right for her. He wasn't a particularly fast runner, and on any other day, Morgan would have driven the ball right past him and into the goal. But this wasn't any ordinary day. Today, Morgan had a tough decision to make. Should she score one for the team, or act as though she weren't as good a soccer player as she knew she could be?

Morgan pulled her leg close to her body and kicked it without much steam. The ball sputtered a few feet. Ryan was able to intercept it with ease. He kicked it down the field toward the goal.

Ryan's footing was unsure. Morgan knew that she could easily outrun him and intercept the ball. But hadn't Hilary warned her not to play better than he did? There was only one thing for her to do. Morgan pretended to trip and fall to the ground. Ryan pulled back his leg and kicked the ball into the goal.

As Morgan stood and wiped the dusty sand from her knees, she took a deep breath. The hurt from the fall was not nearly as painful as her injured pride. There was nothing worse than pretending you were a loser. She didn't even want to think about what Nick and the other guys would have thought if they'd seen that one. They would have known she'd thrown the goal. And that was about as uncool as you could possibly get.

Still, if this could get Ryan to notice her, maybe it would be worth it.

"Good one, Ryan," Morgan congratulated him. She looked straight at the ground. Somehow, Morgan could not bring herself to look Ryan in the eye.

"Tough play," Ryan acknowledged.

Morgan smiled, but in her heart, she knew it hadn't been a tough play at all. "Yeah, good game," she said with as much enthusiasm as she could muster.

"Thanks."

As Morgan walked off the field to the showers she felt uncomfortable with what she had done—especially because she hadn't gotten the reaction from Ryan that she had hoped for. He noticed me all right, she thought. He noticed that I'm a total goof.

CHAPTER FIVE

MR. SMOOTH

Morgan wasn't the only one with romance on her mind. The next day at school, Coleman and Elliott were scouting out groups of girls, looking for that special someone to talk to. It was weird. When they were younger, Coleman and Elliott had had no problem talking to girls. They were just other little kids who happened to wear dresses. But now, here they were in junior high, and suddenly Elliott and

Coleman were trying to plan every word, and every move, just to make the girls like them. Times sure had changed.

Coleman spotted a small group of girls gathered by the soda machine in the school hallway. They looked a few years older than Coleman and Elliott, and that made them a little scary.

"There's one," Coleman said finally, pointing toward a tall girl with long blond hair, wearing a pink sweater and flared jeans. She looked at least two years older than Coleman and Elliott. "Go talk to her."

Elliott gulped. "*You* go talk to her."

Coleman shook his head. "How about we both pick a girl and talk to her."

That sounded like a good idea to Elliot. He reached out his hand to shake on it.

The boys walked hesitantly up toward

the group of girls. Elliott stood near the girl in the pink sweater and looked up at her. She was a good three inches taller than he was.

"Hi. I'm Elliott Rifkin."

The girl in the pink sweater did not even acknowledge the short, red-haired ninth grader who had just spoken to her. She went on gossiping with her friends.

Elliott thought perhaps the girl didn't hear him. So this time he waved his hand to get her attention and spoke loudly. "HI! I'M ELLIOTT!"

The girl heard him that time. In fact, just about everyone in the hall heard him. The girl was so startled by Elliott's announcement that she jumped and spilled her soda—all over Elliott's head.

As the cold, brown, sugary liquid poured down Elliott's face, the group of girls exploded with laughter. Elliott's face turned red as he brushed the soda from his hair, face, and shirt. "Sorry. Can I buy you another . . . uh . . ." Elliott licked his hand and tasted the soda. ". . . root beer?"

The girl in the pink sweater watched with disgust as Elliott licked the sticky soda from his hands. "Uh, no thanks," she told him as she joined the laughter of her friends.

Elliott was totally dejected. He slumped away, hoping no one else in the hall had seen what had just happened. But no such luck. As Elliott walked off, he spotted Coleman, doubled over with laughter. Elliott shot him a dirty look.

Coleman stood tall, fixed the collar on his rugby shirt, and strutted toward the same group of girls Elliott had just left behind. He was determined to show Elliott exactly how this talking to girls thing was done. He sauntered confidently over beside a girl in a green dress and smiled his most dashing grin.

"So, come here often?" he asked the girl. He'd heard that line in a TV movie once.

The girl in the green dress rolled her eyes toward the ceiling. "Duh! We're at school. I come here every day!" She gave Coleman a dirty look and hurried off down the hall.

As the girl moved away from Coleman, he smiled and gave her a little wave. Then he walked over toward Elliott.

"That was totally lame," Elliott chided Coleman.

Coleman shrugged his shoulder. "Maybe next time, I'll try your suave approach," he told Elliott sarcastically, looking at his pal's root beer-stained shirt.

Coleman jumped up and down and waved his arms wildly, like some monster who had finally been set free. "HI! I'M COLEMAN!" he shouted, imitating Elliott. "AARRRGGGH."

Elliott blushed again.

Just then, Coleman spotted a girl with big brown eyes walking down the hall. She was beautiful! Coleman decided to give girls another try. He raced off in her direction.

Elliott watched as Coleman spoke to the girl. He wanted to hear what his friend was saying, but the hallway was too crowded and noisy. Finally, Coleman walked away from the girl. As he passed by Elliott he whispered, "Gonna buy her a soda."

"How'd you do that?" Ellliott asked, impressed.

"Guess I'm just a ladies' man."

Coleman bought the soda, and walked it over to the girl with the brown eyes. She smiled, and took a sip. Elliott moved over and tried to eavesdrop.

"So, great talking to you," Coleman said. As he caught sight of Elliott moving ever closer he suddenly seemed a little nervous. He tried to leave. "See you in biology."

But the girl blocked his path. "Hey, where's my dollar?" she demanded.

Coleman looked nervously from Elliott to the girl. He pretended not to know what she was talking about.

"You said you'd give me a dollar if I let you buy me a soda," the girl reminded Coleman.

Elliott couldn't help laughing as Coleman fished into his pocket, pulled out a crumpled dollar bill, and handed it to the girl.

"Smooth, real smooth," Elliott whispered in Coleman's ear.

CHAPTER SIX

WHY DID I DO THAT?

After the game was over, the soccer players left the field and went home. But
Morgan stayed behind. She grabbed a
bunch of soccer balls and began kicking
them toward the goal. She was the only
one on the field, and that suited her just
fine. She wanted to kick a ball around by
herself. Actually, what she really wanted
to do was kick herself. What had made
her think that blowing that goal and

falling flat on her face was ever going to get Ryan to like her? Now he obviously thought she was a dork, her team had lost the game, and she felt lousy. Morgan kept playing that afternoon's game over and over in her head. And it always came down to the same question: How could she have ever acted so dumb?!

One thing was for sure: Morgan really didn't want to talk to anybody after what had happened that afternoon. And that explained why she was less than thrilled to see her cousin Nick walk on to the field.

"Where have you been?" Nick asked her.

Morgan didn't even look up. She just kept staring at the ground and kicking the ball back and forth between her feet. "Here. Practicing. Got scrimmage tomorrow," she mumbled.

Nick nodded. "I heard that Ryan guy really smoked you in the game today."

Oh great, Morgan thought. *Now everybody knows.* "Yeah, he did," she admitted finally. "That's what I get for listening to Hilary."

Nick shook his head. He knew from experience that doing anything his sister suggested was a bad idea. "Take my advice. Don't listen to Hilary."

Morgan kicked the soccer ball to Nick. And for a while, the two cousins were silent, focusing on moving the ball across the field. Finally, Morgan spoke.

"Guys like her," she said of Hilary. "Playing the helpless female seems to work."

Nick was astounded. "You think losing will make him like you?" he asked incredulously.

Morgan shrugged. "Could you like a girl who beat you at sports?"

Nick didn't answer right away. But after he'd thought about Morgan's question for a while, he nodded. "Sure," he said simply. "If she was nice and could kick game-winning goals. Or run as fast me. A girl like that would be a blast to hang out with."

Morgan laughed despite herself. Nick was talking about her, and trying to make her feel better. He really was a good cousin. And a good friend.

"Too bad Ryan's not as enlightened as you," she told him with a grin.

Nick hadn't always been so generous about Morgan's sports prowess. When she'd first come to town he hadn't been too comfortable with his girl cousin being able to match him point for point in sports. But he'd come around.

"Thanks, Nick."

"Hey, I'll be cheering for you tomorrow," he assured her as he pulled back and slammed the soccer ball down the field.

Later that night, as Morgan walked into her bedroom, she looked up at her poster of Cobi Jones, the midfielder for the Los Angeles Galaxy soccer team. Cobi was an all-star pro known for his speed and explosiveness in the game. And, as Morgan often noticed, he was also kind of cute, with those cool dreadlocks that moved around his head as he ran up and down the field.

Morgan smiled at the poster and pretended to flirt with Cobi Jones just the way Hilary had shown her to. "Oh, Cobi, you're so funny," she said, placing her hands beside her cheek and batting her eyelashes. Morgan laughed despite how rotten she felt. After all, the idea of talking to Cobi Jones that way was so ridiculous there was nothing else to do but laugh, despite Morgan's gloomy mood.

As Morgan got ready for bed, she tried hard not to think about the game the next day. It was going to be hard for her to face her teammates after she'd thrown the game like that. Of course the girls didn't know that Morgan had thrown the game, but Morgan did. In some ways, that made it all the worse.

CHAPTER SEVEN

SURPRISE!

It took Morgan a long time to fall asleep that night. But when she did, she slept soundly. So soundly, in fact, that by the time the next morning came around, she could barely move. But someone insisted on shaking her awake.

"Mom . . . five more minutes . . ." Morgan murmured as she pulled her covers closer around her.

But Morgan's mom wasn't the one

trying to rouse her. In fact, it wasn't any person at all. Morgan was being shaken by an oversized, woolen, blue-and-yellow football jersey, that had once belonged to Morgan and Nick's grandfather.

Now the empty sports sweater was floating around Morgan's room, as though it had come alive! That was totally new. None of the MNFC members had ever seen the jersey do anything on its own— never mind fly! Still, when you are talking about a magical football jersey that can morph kids into pro ball players, you have to expect all sorts of totally weird things to happen.

When Morgan finally opened her eyes, there was a flash of light, like lightning shooting across the room. The brightness of the light startled Morgan. Suddenly she felt the scratchy wool of the magic jersey draped around her shoulders. Morgan jumped. The jersey! How did that get there? The last time Morgan had seen it, the sweater had been folded neatly on the bookshelf in Nick's family room. Had it flown by itself to Morgan's house? Morgan shivered. This jersey was a very scary thing!

Suddenly, everything appeared to go into slow-mo. Morgan held her arm up to her face. Her skin had turned as clear as water. She could see inside her body. The veins and arteries were now clear, and so was her blood. Morgan watched the blood flow through her, and then, without warning, her hand and then arm disappeared completely. Her other arm followed rapidly. Then Morgan felt a disturbing lightness as her legs disappeared beneath her. She was too frightened to even scream.

THE JERSEY

• • •

"Whoa!" Morgan gasped as she ducked out of the way of on an oncoming soccer ball. Huh? The last thing Morgan remembered, she had been safely tucked away in her bed. Now all this weird stuff was happening.

Morgan looked around the field in amazement. This was a big soccer stadium, not some little school field. And what a difference that made. It was a beautiful playing field—with none of the dusty dirt or lumps and bumps that her school field had.

Morgan looked up at the stands. There were so many people there. And they were loud. They were screaming with excitement for the game to begin. Morgan knew that feeling. Every time she was in the crowd at a sporting event, she was filled with anticipation. Now she knew what that sounded like from the player's point of view.

But how did she get here? Somewhere in her fuzzy memory she suddenly recalled feeling the scratchy material of her grandfather's jersey on her shoulders. And the next thing she knew, she was here, in the middle of this soccer stadium. This was exactly like what Nick said about that time he'd turned into Steve Young!

Whoa! The magic jersey had taken her to a real-life soccer game! This was totally amazing. Nick had told her the story of becoming Steve Young about a million times. But Morgan had never been completely sure he was telling the truth. Now here she was, in the middle of a soccer field, and just a few minutes ago she had been in her bed.

Her bed. Oh no! Morgan looked down to make sure she wasn't standing in front of all of these people in her nightgown. Phew! Luckily, she was dressed in a soccer uniform that was the same color as that of the other players on one of the teams. It looked like a Galaxy uniform.

As she looked down at her legs, Morgan was amazed. They were huge, and thick, and hairy! So were her arms. Morgan didn't know what soccer player she had become—but whoever she was, she was a man!

Suddenly an announcer's voice came over the loud speaker. "And last year's number one draft pick for the Los Angeles Galaxy—Clint Mathis!"

Morgan's heart gave a leap. Clint Mathis! He was one of the greatest midfielders in pro soccer. Morgan practiced for hours trying to copy his passing style.

"Clint Mathis! Where?" she asked as she looked around.

Suddenly cameras started flashing everywhere. "Clint! Over here," one reporter called. Morgan looked to see where the reporter was looking. A flashbulb went off, hurting her eyes. But she wasn't so blinded by the lights that she couldn't recognize the muscular soccer star who ran up beside her.

"Cobi Jones!" Morgan exclaimed. "I don't believe it! I have your poster in my bedroom."

Cobi looked confused—and a little weirded-out by his teammate's sudden show of affection. "I'm flattered . . . sort of," he replied.

"Man, this is totally awesome," Morgan continued.

"If you say so," Cobi replied. "Come on. Game time."

"Sure," Morgan told him. "Uh, Cobi? Where am I?"

Cobi started laughing. He thought it was a joke. "Earth. We're on planet Earth." Cobi shook his head and ran for his position.

Morgan just stared at him. Then, one of the scrimmage soccer balls bounced off her head. Whoa! That ball was hit hard, Morgan thought as she rubbed her scalp. Then she shook her head with embarrassment—because it reminded her of the first time she had spoken to Ryan—when she'd gotten him in the head with a ball. And look what a mess *that* had gotten her into!

Cobi Jones came by and grabbed Morgan by the shoulders. "Okay, Mathis. You're in New York," Cobi said. "You're playing against the Metro Stars. You gonna get your head into the game?"

Mathis? Morgan stared at Cobi in surprise. Oh, man! She was inside Clint Mathis's body. How awesome! Wait until the guys in the MNFC heard about this one!

Lots of kids would be totally freaked out at the prospect of having soccer balls kicked at them from all directions at top speed by professional soccer players. But not Morgan. Of course it helped that Nick had already been inside the body of a professional athlete before her. At least she was somewhat prepared for the prospect. And she also knew a lot about soccer—so the rules and some of the plays probably wouldn't throw her. In fact, Morgan had to admit that the idea of playing major league soccer left her totally psyched!

This was all of her dreams coming true—and she didn't even have to wait until she grew up for it to happen!

Just to prove how psyched she was, Morgan started to excite the crowd. She waved to them, and urged them to cheer louder. The crowd was under Morgan's spell—especially since they believed she was Clint Mathis. They followed Clint's directions and screamed louder, louder, and louder!

"Awright!" Morgan cheered from inside Clint Mathis's skin, as she looked out at the adoring soccer fans. "These boys can eat my dust!"

CHAPTER EIGHT

BOYS WILL BE BOYS

At the very moment that Morgan (as Clint Mathis) was taking practice shots on the New York Metro Stars' home field, her fellow MNFC members were busy having a whole new experience of their own. And in some ways, what was happening with the boys was even weirder than what Morgan was going through.

Nick, Elliott, and Coleman were reading Hilary's teen girl magazines!

"When applying eyeliner never pull down on the lid. You may create permanent wrinkles." Coleman looked up from the page he was reading out loud. "I had no idea being a girl was so complicated," he told his buds.

"The more I read, the more confused I get," Nick admitted.

Elliott looked at his pale, freckled skin in the mirror. "I found out I'm an autumn," Elliott told the other boys, referring to a system in which clothing is divided into four groups of colors, and each group is given the name of a season. In Elliott's case that season was autumn because of his red hair, light skin, and freckles. "I should wear rust tones and deep blues. What do you think?"

Nick snorted. "I think you're losing your mind." He glanced through the table of contents of another one of Hilary's magazines. But that one didn't have the information he was looking for, either.

"Any luck?" Coleman asked.

Nick shook his head. "Nope. Unless you want to know the Backstreet Boys' turn-ons and turn-offs."

Elliott glanced away from the mirror. "What're their turn-offs?" he asked in all seriousness.

"Phonies and global warming," Nick read from the magazine.

"Mine, too!" Elliott said excitedly.

Coleman laughed. Then he pointed to a column in yet another of Hilary's seemingly endless pile of advice and fashion magazines. "Here's something I've seen in two magazines. It must be true. It says girls like guys who have a sense of humor."

Elliott grinned proudly and pointed toward himself. "I'm funny."

"Looking," Nick added sarcastically.

"Well, you should talk," Elliott replied.

Nick walked toward Coleman and read over his shoulder. "Also, they seem to like guys with abs of steel."

Coleman stood up and patted his stomach. "Check," he bragged.

"Yeah, right," Elliott said with a laugh as he tried to imagine how he would look in a light blue T-shirt instead of the yellow one he was wearing at the moment. Then he turned to his friends. "You know, I saw in a movie once that girls like bad boys."

The three boys stood and walked around the room, trying to imitate movie tough guys. They scrunched their faces, narrowed their eyes, and sized up the imaginary enemy in Nick's family room.

"We're bad," Nick vowed as he scrunched up his mouth, put his hands in his pockets, and hunched over just slightly.

"Uh-huh," Coleman agreed, taking on a similar pose. "We're pretty good at this stuff."

Elliott didn't add anything. He was busy practicing being the strong, silent type. One of the magazines had reported that girls liked guys who were like that.

The guys were so busy practicing their bad boy personas that they didn't even notice that Hilary had walked into the room. She was dressed as her Lola character for a rehearsal of *Damn Yankees*. She wore a skintight black leotard, her hair was piled high on top of her head, and she wore a red baseball cap. She had also applied a lot of makeup.

"What are you three stooges up to?"

she asked the boys in a voice that was definitely not as friendly as her Lola voice.

The boys were too amazed at Hilary's appearance to reply. They had never seen her dressed that grown-up before. It was quite a shock. All they could do was stare at her.

"Never mind," she said finally. She turned to Nick. "Tell Mom I'm at rehearsal."

Elliott broke the silence. "Hey, Hilary, wanna hear a joke?" he asked, trying to see if girls really did like guys with a sense of humor.

"Coming from you guys, that would be redundant," Hilary told Elliott.

What a slam!

"Good one, Elliott," Coleman laughed at his friend's feeble attempt.

"Tough room," Elliott admitted.

CHAPTER NINE

TOO MANY QUESTIONS, TOO LITTLE TIME

Morgan was going through some strange times of her own. It was hard enough to adjust to being somebody else—one of the best players in professional soccer, no less! But to have to do it in front of thousands of screaming people, and lots of other muscular professional soccer players made it a little difficult.

Morgan was determined to make the most of this situation, however. She had a million questions she wanted to ask Cobi Jones. Some of them were about certain plays he'd perfected on the field—and others were of a more "personal" nature. But the game was about to start, and Morgan didn't have much time. She decided to ask Cobi the most important question first.

"Would you like a girl who could beat you at soccer?" she asked quickly.

Cobi looked curiously at the person he thought was his friend, Clint Mathis. What kind of question was *that* for one grown man to ask another? He thought about it for a few seconds. "Uh, sure, why not?" he answered finally.

Morgan smiled triumphantly. "I knew it. This is the last time I listen to Hilary," she declared.

Cobi seemed confused. "Who's Hilary?

And why are we talking about this now?"

Morgan was so pleased with Cobi's answer that she completely forgot she was now in Clint Mathis's body. She had a million questions to ask him, and they all started pouring out of her mouth. "What about girls who laugh at everything you say?" she asked Cobi. "Do you like that?"

"The game's starting, Mathis," Cobi reminded his teammate.

That comment knocked Morgan back to reality. She wasn't Morgan anymore, she was Clint Mathis—at least for the time being. And her problems didn't matter now. The team did. Winning did. And for the first time since she had met Ryan on the scrimmage field, Morgan felt excitement and enthusiasm for the game of soccer. "Cool!" she exclaimed. "I'm ready to play."

Cobi seemed puzzled. "Then why aren't you in position?" He asked.

Oops!

"Oh, yeah," Morgan said as she trotted off toward her position. "We'll talk about girls after the game, okay?"

Morgan raced over to the starting position. Suddenly, as she eyed the opposing players from across the field, all thoughts of Ryan, flirting, and questions flew right out of her head. There was only one thing on her mind—making sure that the black-and-white soccer ball went into the opposing team's goal, and stayed out of her own.

The ref blew the whistle and the game began. The players were kicking the ball harder than Morgan ever could've imagined. It flew through the air at rapid-fire speed. The players kicked the ball back and forth to one another so quickly that it was hard to keep track of who had it at any given time. This was the big leagues!

And yet, Morgan wasn't the least bit afraid. She knew she was in the body of Clint Mathis, and that made her stronger and faster than many of the players on the field.

Cobi Jones kicked the ball right in Morgan's direction. Morgan was ready to receive it. She reached out her foot, stopped the ball, and then quickly took it down the field. The Metro Stars were no slouches. They took after her at top speed. But Morgan instinctively used passing skills she'd never even known about to get the ball around the Metro Stars players and over to her Galaxy teammates.

All around her, Morgan could hear the crowd roaring. The enthusiasm that the players felt for their sport was infectious. The crowd had caught the fire. Their cheers gave her an energy she never knew she had. Quickly, she dodged away from an oncoming Metro Stars defender and headed toward the goal cage.

Boy, I have to remember these moves, she thought to herself as she got in scoring position.

A Galaxy forward gave the ball a swift bicycle kick in Morgan's direction. The ball soared high in the air. Morgan stood beneath it, ready to receive.

Morgan jumped up high and kicked the ball.

For a minute, all action seemed to stop. In Morgan's mind, it was like the ball was moving through the air in slow motion. Would it go in the goal, or would it be intercepted . . .?

SCORE!

Whoa! The ball had sailed right into the goal cage. Morgan had done it! She'd scored the very first goal of the game. Wait until the guys in the MNFC heard about this one!

Morgan grinned as her Galaxy teammates high-fived her—all the time thinking she was Clint Mathis, of course.

Without a doubt, this had to be one of the best days of her life.

CHAPTER TEN

NICK'S DISCOVERY

It was too bad things weren't going quite as well for the rest of the MNFC gang that afternoon. They were all getting pretty confused by the information they had discovered in Hilary's magazines.

"We should run all this stuff by Morgan to make sure these magazines aren't trying to trick us," Elliot said as he looked at the pile in front of him.

Coleman looked curiously at Elliott.

"Why would they do that?" he asked.

Elliott shrugged. "Women are weird. They do weird things. Like they put on all this makeup so they can look natural." He opened one of the magazines and pointed to an article called "Get That Natural Look." It listed ten different kinds of makeup that teenage girls should wear to look as though they weren't wearing any makeup at all.

Nick glanced at the article and scowled. It was obvious to him that no real girl would ever get up extra early each morning to curl her hair, cover her eyes with mascara, and make sure that her eye shadow matched her lipstick. After all, Morgan didn't do any of that. He was sure of it. "Morgan looks natural," he pointed out to his friends.

"Maybe she wears makeup," Elliott suggested.

Coleman laughed. "So what does she look like without makeup? *Unnatural?*" he argued with Elliott.

Nick tossed his pile of magazines to the den floor in frustration. "Can we talk about something else?" he said finally. He'd had all he could take of makeup, fashion, diets, and the true secrets of famous pop stars. "Where is Morgan, anyway?"

Elliott sighed. "What'd I tell you? It's happening just like I said. She's breaking away from us. She's moving on."

Nick threw a pillow at Elliott's head. That was not something he even wanted to think about. "Shut up!" he ordered. "She'll be here. She's got soccer scrimmage later today."

But Elliott wasn't convinced. "Call me crazy . . ."

"You're crazy," Coleman told him with a laugh.

Elliott frowned. "I wasn't finished. I was about to say call me crazy, but I can't see what Morgan and all these girls see in that Ryan guy."

Nick and Coleman looked at Elliott and shrugged. They didn't know either. They'd never actually thought about it before.

Elliott stood up, looked in the mirror, and brushed his hands through his thick, short hair. "He's no autumn," he assured himself.

Elliott checked out his looks in the mirror and worried about what girls his age were looking for in a man. He stood as tall as he could and brushed his hair down on his forehead to see if that would make him look older and more attractive.

At the same time, Coleman stood firm

and began flexing his abdominal muscles, trying to give himself those muscle-bound abs that the magazines said girls liked. In his mind, he began to practice all sorts of great pick-up lines he could use to introduce himself to the girls at school.

As Nick watched his friends study themselves in the hopes of impressing girls, he was getting more than a little grossed-out. He didn't see what the big deal was. He decided that if you had to go through all that to get a girl, she probably wasn't worth getting in the first place.

Nick decided to change the subject. Quickly he stood up and walked toward the bookshelf, looking for a book called *Plays of the Football Pros*. Maybe he and the guys could try out a few moves. He needed to read something he could understand.

Coleman agreed. "If these magazines are right, then we are totally clueless, " he told the others.

Nick began looking for his book. As he scanned the shelves, he suddenly realized something had disappeared.

"I don't believe it!" Nick exclaimed. "The jersey's missing!"

Nick was in shock. He knew he had left the jersey right on the third shelf. He *always* kept the jersey in the den. That was where the MNFC met.

"What?" Elliott gasped.

"You sure?" Coleman asked.

Nick didn't take the time to answer. He had a feeling he knew what had happened to the jersey. He picked up the phone and began dialing his Aunt April's phone number.

"Hi, Aunt April," Nick said into the receiver as soon as Morgan's mother answered. "Could I talk to Morgan?"

Coleman and Elliott moved closer to the phone, hoping to pick up some of what Nick's aunt was saying.

"Not there, huh?" Nick continued. "Do you know where she went? No? Well, thanks."

As Nick hung up the phone, his face got red with anger. The jersey was missing, and so was Morgan. That was enough circumstantial evidence to prove that she had stolen it. Ever since Nick had told her that he had become Steve Young, he knew that Morgan wanted to try and "jump" into the body of a famous sports star. And considering the way she was feeling about her soccer skills these days, Morgan had probably hoped that putting on the jersey would turn her into some famous soccer player.

Nick wasn't sure that the jersey would work if it were worn by anyone else, and neither was Morgan. And no one knew if the jersey would work on command. But Nick was pretty sure that Morgan had been desperate enough to steal the jersey and give it a try.

And *that* was against the rules. Nobody in the MNFC was supposed to take the jersey without telling him. It was his jersey after all.

"The jersey's gone and Morgan's gone!" Nick exploded. "I can't believe she jumped!"

"Women!" Elliott exclaimed. "You can never tell *what* they are gonna do!"

CHAPTER ELEVEN

JUST DO IT!

Morgan looked up at the scoreboard as she kicked the ball down toward the Metro Stars goal. The game was tied at one goal apiece. There was only a minute left in the game. It was now or never. Cobi Jones ran up beside her. Morgan tapped the ball with her foot and deftly passed it right to him.

"Go for it, Clint," Cobi said breathlessly. "I'm gonna set you up. And you're gonna punch it with a scissor kick."

JUST DO IT!

For the first time since she'd jumped into Clint Mathis's body, Morgan seemed a little unsure of herself. The whole game was resting on her shoulders. "I'll try," she told Cobi.

Cobi stared incredulously at his buddy Clint. "You'll try?!" he asked in disbelief. "This is what you do! Just kick it like you know how."

"Okay," Morgan said, but as Clint's voice came out of her mouth, it sounded doubtful.

"Know it. Believe it. Do it!" Cobi told her.

Morgan took a deep breath. She gathered her confidence. "Get that ball to me," she told Cobi finally, as she ran toward the goal.

Cobi gave the ball a strong kick in Morgan's direction. The Metro Stars defenders surrounded her, trying to intercept the ball. But Morgan was ready. She dove through the circle of opposing players and got her foot on the ball. With one strong scissor kick she sent the ball smashing in the direction of the goal cage and watched as it flew right past the goalie.

SCORE!

Morgan couldn't believe it! She had won the game! She reached out and high-fived Cobi.

A throng of reporters surrounded the two players, shoving microphones and cameras in their faces.

"What was that last move, Cobi?" one reporter asked.

"I just set up Clint, 'cause I knew he'd make the goal. It's just what he does."

The reporter turned his mike in Morgan's direction.

"Clint, anything to add?"

"Yeah," Morgan replied. "I knew I was Clint Mathis, so I could totally do it! And it didn't matter if guys didn't like me and Hilary's wrong, anyway, and . . ."

The looks on the reporters' faces made Morgan realize what she had just said. Those were not the words of a professional soccer player! Those were the words of a junior high school girl. A very embarrassed junior high school girl!

"Hey, we won, didn't we?" Morgan said finally. She raised her arm in victory.

A group of fans raced onto the field. One of them grabbed Clint Mathis's soccer jersey. Suddenly Morgan felt like everything was moving in slow motion. The minute the fan had tugged at Clint's jersey, Morgan began morphing back into herself. Shiny lights circled around Clint

Mathis's body. Suddenly, Morgan felt a lightness in her arms. She held her hand in front of her face. The skin had turned clear. The blood was transparent as well, and Morgan could see it oozing its way through her veins and arteries. She looked down at her feet, but they had already disappeared. It seemed to Morgan that everything was happening in slow motion, but that wasn't so. In fact, time was moving faster than Morgan could imagine. So fast that no one at the stadium even noticed that Morgan was being morphed back from a professional soccer player to a normal kid—one who had just lived out her ultimate fantasy!

And then it was over. Morgan was back in her bedroom, wearing the scratchy old football jersey. She sat there on the bed for a moment, clutching her arms around her, and trying to contemplate what had just happened to her. Not only had she played a pro soccer game, she'd won the game for her team. And she'd gotten to meet Cobi Jones. Of course, he'd thought she was Clint Mathis at the time, but that was cool. After all, Morgan knew what had just happened, and she had learned lessons she would never forget.

Clint Mathis, however, had absolutely no memories of the game. He had no idea that he had scored the winning goal, or that he had asked his pal Cobi Jones a few questions that were definitely out of character for him. And he certainly didn't know that a junior high school girl named Morgan had entered his body.

As Clint stared in confusion at the cheering fans and the reporters, Cobi sidled up beside him. "You did it, Clint," he congratulated his teammate. "Now we can talk about girls."

Clint shrugged. "Sure, if that's what you want to do," he told Cobi. "What girls do you want to talk about?"

Now Cobi was *really* confused. Didn't Clint remember their pre-game conversation? Cobi sighed. Obviously his pal Clint must've taken one too many soccer balls to the head.

Morgan sat on her bed and looked up at her poster of Cobi Jones. We did it, she thought. We won the game!

Morgan had to admit that winning that soccer game was the biggest thrill she'd ever had. Not even a smile from Ryan would ever measure up to knowing that she had played her best and helped bring the Galaxy to victory.

Just then her bedroom door flung open. Her cousin Nick was standing in the doorway.

"You jumped!" Nick accused Morgan with an angry tone to his voice. He could see that she was wearing the jersey, and he didn't like the idea.

"The jersey must've followed me home," Morgan told her cousin. "That thing is so weird."

"You can explain later," Nick assured her. "But right now, you have a game to play."

Morgan picked up her watch from her night table. That Galaxy game had gone on for a long time! It was almost 3:00 in the afternoon! She had a soccer scrimmage in just a few minutes. Quickly, Morgan reached over the side of the bed and pulled out her shin guards and wrapped them around her legs. "Yeah. And this one's gonna be a little bit different," she assured her cousin as she adjusted the Velcro.

Nick thought about what his cousin had just told him. "The jersey followed you home?" he asked her in disbelief. That was the first time anything like that had ever happened with the jersey. Yikes! If the jersey actually had a mind of its own, that meant that there was no controlling when, where, or which sports superstar the MNFC members might wind up becoming.

But there was no time to think about that right now. Morgan had to get going. She had a scrimmage to play in.

CHAPTER TWELVE

YOU DESERVE A BREAK TODAY

By the time Nick and Morgan reached the soccer field, the teams were already practicing. Coleman and Elliott were on the sidelines, staring at another group of girls.

"I have a new concept to try," Elliott told Coleman.

Coleman watched as Elliott approached two girls. Elliott turned to a girl with big brown eyes and smiled brightly.

"Hi. I couldn't help noticing you have

such great eyes. I just felt I had to tell you," Elliott said, mustering as much confidence as he could.

"Thanks," the girl replied sweetly.

Elliott was shocked. This actually seemed to be working! "Yeah. I mean . . . you're welcome," he stammered.

"Boy, I hope you're still this nice after you get out of elementary school," the girl continued as she walked away.

Elementary school? Elliott was mortified. How could she think he was still in elementary school? Couldn't she tell how mature he was?

Coleman had heard the whole thing. He felt pretty bad for Elliott. "I didn't think her eyes were that pretty, anyway," he remarked, trying to comfort his pal, as Elliott slumped back to where Coleman was standing.

Morgan and Nick came running over toward the field. They stopped to catch their breath beside Elliott and Coleman. Just then, Ryan came trotting by. "Hey, Morgan, I'll give you a break today. How's that?" he called over to her.

Morgan gave Nick a knowing grin. Nick laughed. When Morgan got through playing her best, Ryan wasn't going to know what hit him!

Morgan took her place on the field. The ref blew the whistle and the game began. As soon as Morgan was able to intercept the ball, she drove downfield. Ryan ran over and tried to steal the ball away, but Morgan moved to her left and faked him out. As she kept running, maintaining complete control of the ball, Ryan stared at her with surprise. This was not what he had been expecting at all.

Morgan was really making the other team sweat. They couldn't keep up with her. At one point Ryan grabbed control of the ball and tried to run toward the girls' team's goal. But Morgan was all over him like a glove. If he dove to the right, she dove to the right. If he dodged to the left, she was right there beside him. And when Ryan kicked the ball toward the goal cage, Morgan reached out her foot and intercepted.

Bam! No goal!

Morgan took the ball down the field as fast as she could. As she neared the goal, she passed it to a teammate who slammed it past the other team's goalie. Right in the pocket!

After that, Ryan was afraid of Morgan's soccer talents. Whenever he got the ball, he made sure to pass it to one of his teammates. He didn't want to risk Morgan intercepting it from him again.

But, of course, Morgan eventually did take control of the ball. She passed it off to a teammate and ran down field at top speed, avoiding the opposing players at every turn. As Morgan got into scoring position, her teammate kicked the ball back to her. That's when Morgan remembered the words Cobi Jones had used to cheer her on when he thought she was Clint Mathis. It had given her the confidence she'd needed then, and it was about to give her the same feeling now.

Know it. Believe it. Do it!

Morgan pulled her leg back and let loose with a powerful scissor kick. The ball soared through the air, right over the goalie's head.

SCORE!

"Got that one from Cobi Jones!" Morgan shouted to her teammates. Then she turned to see Ryan. His hands were resting on his thighs as he bent over to catch his breath.

"Hey, Ryan!" she called to him, sarcastically. "Thanks for the break."

Ryan looked up at Morgan. His breathing was heavy and labored from trying to outrun Morgan. He was too winded to even respond to her sarcasm.

By the time the final whistle blew, Morgan's team had won the game, three goals to zero.

"Great game!" the goalie from Morgan's team congratulated her. "You blew 'em away girl!"

Morgan smiled. "I was just playing like I knew how."

"Yeah. And not listening to Hilary's stupid advice," Nick said as he, Coleman, and Elliott came over to congratulate Morgan.

"I picked up a few moves when I jumped," she whispered to the other members of the MNFC. They were the only ones who would ever understand what Morgan meant by jumping. She turned and looked Nick straight in the eye. "Listen Nick, I didn't swipe the jersey. I swear. I was asleep and it woke me up!"

"Weird," Nick replied. "That thing is creepy, but sometimes it seems like it has a point." He shook his head, realizing what he had just said. If that were true, then the jersey would actually have to have a mind of its own. And that was impossible, wasn't it? Of course, up until a few weeks ago he had always thought it was impossible to enter another person's body. And he wasn't so sure. Still, a jersey that could move on its own . . . ? "Never mind. That's crazy," he added quickly. But his voice didn't seem very certain.

"Hey, anything's possible," Morgan told him.

Elliott shook his head. One thing didn't seem to be possible, as far as he was concerned. No girls were going to like him. At least not for now.

"I've made up my mind. My health sciences teacher said girls mature faster than boys. So that means I've got some time to catch up. Then they'll be all over me," he declared.

"Elliott, you scare me more than the jersey!" Morgan laughed as she ran off to gather up her stuff.

"Hey, Morgan! Wait up!"

Just then, Morgan heard a familiar voice calling to her from across the field. It was Ryan!

"You were really tearing it up out there today," he told Morgan as he trotted up alongside her.

"Yeah."

"I was wondering," Ryan began shyly, "if you wanted to, um, hang out later?"

Morgan glanced over at her cousin and his friends. They were all goofing on Elliott and laughing. They looked like they were really having fun. "Maybe," she told Ryan finally. "But not now. I've got something I gotta do with my friends."

As Morgan ran over to join Nick, Elliott, and Coleman, she knew Ryan was watching her. From the corner of her eye, she saw two girls go over and start to flirt with him. But Morgan knew Ryan wasn't paying attention to them.

I am sooo loving my life right now, Morgan thought happily to herself.

CHAPTER THIRTEEN

NOT AGAIN?

"Aaaahhhh!"

Elliott came slamming off the top of a hill on the BMX bike trail. His screams filled the air. But Elliott was smiling as he screamed. These days, Elliott seemed a little braver. After talking to those girls, nothing seemed scary.

As Elliott reached the bottom of the hill, he waited with Coleman and Morgan as Nick powered himself up a hill. "I'm gonna make it this time," Nick shouted down to his friends, as he nodded in the direction of a huge mud puddle.

Nick revved his bike up to top speed as he reached the top of the hill. Then he rode off the edge and soared through the air. His friends held their breath and then . . .

Nick cleared the puddle! He flashed his friends a triumphant grin and raised his arm in victory as he rode by his friends.

"Nick! Look out!" Morgan screamed.

Nick looked back at Morgan. Then he glanced a few feet ahead of himself—just in time to realize that he was heading for disaster. He hit a small rise in the trail and flipped off his bike. *Splash!* Nick had landed in yet another mud puddle.

Morgan couldn't hold back her laughter as she found Nick sitting in a pile of sticky black mud once again. She ran over and sat beside him on dry land.

"Oh, Nick!" she said sarcastically, batting her eyelashes at him and imitating the girls who had flirted with Ryan. "You're so brave!"

Nick scowled and threw a huge handful of mud at Morgan. She laughed hysterically, hopped back on her bike, and rode back up the hill. She was going to show those boys how BMX biking was really done!

"Women!" Coleman and Elliott exclaimed as they watched her climb higher and higher.

FROM THE JERSEY #3
NICK'S A CHICK

CHAPTER ONE

LOW MAN ON THE
PRIMATE TOTEM POLE

"KREEE! KREEE!" Nick Lighter shouted, waving his arms. "Larry Byrd! The Byrd Man *swoops* down, steals the pass, makes a fast break to the bucket, and . . ."

"In your dreams, Lighter!" his cousin Morgan yelled back, catching him off-guard and grabbing the ball. "Lisa Leslie's unstoppable! She leaps, she shoots. . . *Slam dunk!*"

Elliott Rifkin, who was Morgan's two-on-two basketball partner, scrunched up his face. "Lisa who?"

Morgan faked a lay-up, then swizzled the ball to Elliottt who tripped on Coleman's shoelace. *Splat!*

"Foul!" cried Elliott.

Coleman grabbed the ball. "Whaddya mean, *foul*?"

Morgan, her hands on her hips, looked at Coleman's sneaker laces, which were snaked around his ankles like limp spaghetti.

"Pathetic. Boys are so lame about the simplest things, like tying shoes. I bet if you did a survey you would find that girls have to retie their shoes a mere fraction of the number of times that boys do!"

"Baloney!" shouted Nick. "Girls Velcro their sneakers closed. Guys . . . *real* guys . . . use laces. Besides, we are playing basketball, not shopping for shoes!"

Morgan had read the riot act to Nick on and off for at least fifteen minutes, and she thought it was about time to read it once again.

"Where on earth did you hear that? In case you haven't noticed, my sneakers are laced, not Velcro-ed. Explain that, why don't you?!"

"Okay, I'll explain it: you're a mutant!"

Coleman helped Elliott to his feet, made him hold out his arms, and then began to trace the air.

Nick butted in, "Are you hypnotizing him?"

Coleman continued to make Elliott follow his finger. "No, this is how you tell if an NBA player is injured. You hold out his hands and then you check his eyes and see if he can follow you. If he can't follow you with his eyes, that means there's something seriously wrong."

Nick stared into Elliott's eyes. "Hey. He does look kinda strange."

Coleman nodded. "That's the trouble. He *always* looks that way."

Nick took the ball out to the sidelines and shot it back to Coleman, but before 'Slaw could lay a finger on it, Morgan grabbed it loose and sank a beautiful hook shot. Coleman looked at her in awe.

"Man! Morgan, you should try out for the school team tomorrow. You're a demon in disguise."

Nick, faking around Elliott added, "Yeah, but that's tomorrow. Right now we're playing basketball! 'Slaw!"

Elliott, nursing a bruised elbow, tried to block Coleman's pass to Nick, only to find himself alone once again at the end of the driveway. Morgan sidestepped Coleman, grabbed the pass, and made another beeline to the basket.

"Lisa Leslie spins, turns, jumps, and makes the three pointer from downtown!"

Elliott's voice rang out, "So who's Lisa Leslie!?"

"Only one of the best players on the WNBA," Morgan yelled back.

Nick dribbled over to Coleman. "Oh, you mean the W-N-R-B-A. That's the *We're Not Really Basketball Association.*"

Morgan sank the ball without even looking. Her focus was on her cousin. "Excuse me, but they can go one-on-one with anybody, thank you very much!"

Coleman took the ball out and shot it back to Nick.

"Women's basketball *is* kinda lame, Morgan. Let's face it. It's a guy's game."

As Nick steadied himself for a shot, he nodded his approval to Coleman. "Everybody knows women aren't as good as men." Morgan's glare froze him solid, until he added, "I mean, at basketball!"

Morgan whomped the ball hard into Nick's chest. "You know, sometimes I really see Mr. Osterman's point about how men are similar to gorillas."

Coleman began to heave with laughter. "Major diss!"

Elliott piped up. "Well, scientifically speaking, she's right. We happen to be only one or two notches above apes on the primate totem pole."

Nick looked at Elliott as if he'd grown another head. "The *what?* What are you talking about?" He steadied himself, fired, and missed the basket by a yard.

Morgan caught the rebound, did a fancy behind-the-back, through-the-legs, over-the-shoulder dribble, then passed it to Elliott, who made a leaping toss and, to everyone's amazement, made the basket. With a huge grin, he turned to Nick.

"Remember when we saw that traveling exhibit at the museum, *The Primate Totem Pole?* Well, the Low Man on the Primate Totem Pole has no brain. From there, you climb the evolutionary ladder to . . ."

Nick interrupted, "The Monday Night Football Club!"

"Ex-actly!" Coleman added enthusiastically.

As he and Elliott and Nick did high-fives, Morgan sank another layup.

"Excuse me, but Lisa Leslie scored a hundred points in the first half of a game in high school. And she can totally knock down the threes! I think that proves something."

Elliott, still triumphant from his one basket, strutted forward in a mock Jamal Anderson Dirty Bird, then put one finger to his temple, as if contacting a mystic spirit. "Actually, with the occasional exception, as noted, what Nick says is basically true. Man is superior to woman. It's a simple scientific fact. Women can't build muscle mass like men, they're generally weaker, not as fast . . ."

Morgan shook her head, returning an icy glare. "Elliott, that is such garbage!"

With lightning speed, she spun on her heels, stole the ball from Nick, and thumped it hard into Elliott, almost knocking the wind out of him. Nick grabbed it on the rebound off Elliott's chest and went one-on-one with her in a grudge match.

Coleman and Elliott suddenly found themselves on the sidelines cheering.

"Go Nick-y! Go!"

"You got it, Morgan, shoot!"

Locked in a dead heat to the basket, Nick was all business, dead serious and intent on winning. Morgan, on the other hand, was a loose goose, laughing, leaping, and out-maneuvering Nick at every turn. She finally stole the ball, drove to the bucket and planted a perfect jump shot.

Coleman nudged his buddy, "Did you see that move?"

Elliott's eyes were glazed over and dreamy. "Yeah, she just sort of floated up to the basket without any effort. She was totally relaxed, poised, and in control."

"I'd say she's ready for the girls' basketball try-outs," Coleman said.

Elliott agreed. "Oh, yeah."

Wiping a few beads of sweat from her brow, Morgan stuck out her neck toward Nick and smiled. "If guys are so much better at sports, how come I can beat all of you?"

Coleman, Elliott, and Nick exchanged vacant glances, then Nick plucked his favorite answer out of thin air: "'Cause you're a mutant!"

THE JERSEY

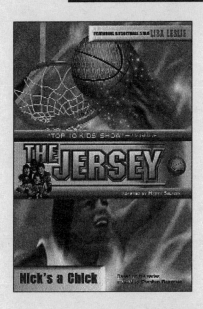

*Nick has always made fun of the WNBA — saying they are not a **real** basketball league*

Find out what happens to Nick when he puts on the jersey and is catapulted into the game as star center Lisa Leslie in . . .

THE JERSEY #3
Nick's a Chick

COMING DOWN THE COURT IN SEPTEMBER 2000

Check out *The Jersey*
on Disney Channel